Marmaduke

IT'S A DOG'S LIFE

by Brad Anderson

TOR

A TOM DOHERTY ASSOCIATES BOOK
NEW YORK

MARMADUKE: IT'S A DOG'S LIFE

Copyright © 1982, 1983, 1989 by United Feature Syndicate, Inc.

A TOR Book®
Published by Tom Doherty Associates, Inc.
49 West 24 Street
New York, NY 10010

ISBN: 0-812-57355-2   Can. ISBN: 0-812-57356-0

First edition: March 1989

Printed in the United States of America

0 9 8 7 6 5 4 3 2 1

© 1982 United Feature Syndicate, Inc.

© 1982 United Feature Syndicate, Inc.

© 1962 United Feature Syndicate, Inc.

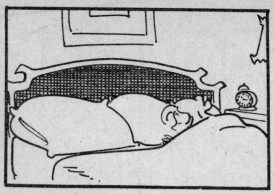

WHOOSH!

© 1982 United Feature Syndicate, Inc.

1-16-83

LOOKS LIKE YOU JUST GOT EVICTED!

SIGHHHH

© 1983 United Feature Syndicate, Inc.

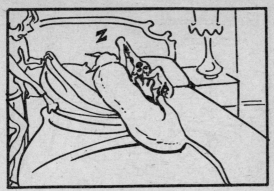

3.6

© 1983 United Feature Syndicate. Inc.

3-13

© 1983 United Feature Syndicate, Inc.

© 1983 United Feature Syndicate, Inc.

© 1983 United Feature Syndicate, Inc.

© 1983 United Feature Syndicate, Inc.

© 1983 United Feature Syndicate, Inc.

LOOK AT THAT! WHENEVER I WANT TO SIT IN MY FAVORITE CHAIR ...HE'S IN IT!

THERE ISN'T ROOM FOR OUR FEET UNDER THE TABLE!

I'M ALWAYS STEPPING OVER HIM!

AND WHEN IT'S TIME FOR BED...

EEEEARRGHH

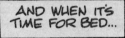

© 1983 United Feature Syndicate, Inc.